RSPCA

Animal  Tales

The Million Paws Puppy

Other books in the
RSPCA ANIMAL TALES series

Ruby's Misadventure
Double Trouble
An Unexpected Arrival

The Million Paws Puppy

Chris Kunz

RANDOM HOUSE AUSTRALIA

A Random House book
Published by Random House Australia Pty Ltd
Level 3, 100 Pacific Highway, North Sydney NSW 2060
www.randomhouse.com.au

First published by Random House Australia in 2012

Addresses for companies within the Random House Group can be
found at www.randomhouse.com.au/offices

National Library of Australia
Cataloguing-in-Publication Entry

Author: Chris Kunz
Title: The million paws puppy/Chris Kunz
ISBN: 978 1 74275 326 3 (pbk)
Series: Animal tales; 1
Target Audience: For primary school age
Subjects: Dogs – Juvenile Fiction
Dewey Number: A823.4

Cover photograph © Patricia Doyle/Getty Images
Cover and internal design by Ingrid Kwong
Internal illustrations by Charlotte Whitby
Internal photographs: image of cat by iStockphoto; image of horse by
Shutterstock; image of dog by Patricia Doyle/Getty Images;
image of terriers by Jerry Young/Getty Images
Typeset by Midland Typesetters, Australia
Printed in Australia by Griffin Press, an accredited ISO AS/NZS
14001:2004 Environmental Management System printer

Random House Australia uses papers that are natural, renewable
and recyclable products and made from wood grown in sustainable
forests. The logging and manufacturing processes are expected to
conform to the environmental regulations of the country of origin.

Chapter One

'Annnnnd . . . jump! Good boy, Ripper, good boy!'

Cassie Bannerman, nine and a half years old and the best dog trainer around, moved the stick up another few centimetres. 'Wait – wait . . . and jump!'

Ripper took off, jumping easily over the

raised stick. He looked back at his owner and grinned, tail wagging energetically. To anyone unfamiliar with Ripper, this grin could be a little intimidating, but Ripper's grin was just like him: strong, warm and open. But a little too open for the little terrier nearby, who took one look at Ripper, squealed and ran behind his owner's legs.

'Attaboy, Ripper,' enthused Cassie, her green eyes sparkling, unaware of the small dog's reaction. Ripper then raced around some witch's hats while Cassie timed him. 'Awesome work, Ripper!'

He wriggled through a plastic tunnel, commando-style, and at the end, brought his paw up to shake hands with Cassie. He drooled happily as she rubbed his chest.

'Such a clever dog! Okay, who's next?' Cassie glanced over at a timid-looking beagle called Henry, who seemed to sense that Ripper's performance was a hard act to follow.

'Off you go, Henry,' encouraged Cassie, tucking her dark brown hair behind her ears.

Henry took off at a sedate pace, dodging the witch's hats and enjoying his owner, Suzy, cheering from the sidelines.

Cassie and Ripper had recently attended RSPCA dog-training classes and quickly became stars of the class. Now she helped other families in the neighbourhood practise their training. She was well known to the pet owners of Abbotts Hill. Her parents owned the local deli and she had grown up familiar with pretty much everyone in the community. And anyone in Abbotts Hill would tell you that Cassie Bannerman didn't go anywhere without an animal close behind.

When she turned six Cassie's family decided to adopt a beautiful little kitten from the local RSPCA shelter. Cassie called him Gladiator and he had grown up to suit his name. He was a large and ferociously playful tabby who spent most of his time in the deli, attacking legs as they passed by the aisle where he often slept.

He had a perfectly good bed in the family home, which was behind the shop, but he wanted to be where the action was. Cassie's parents had even put a 'Beware of the Cat' sign on their shop wall, but new customers mistakenly thought it was a joke!

By the time Cassie was seven, she was desperate for a dog. And after another visit to the RSPCA, she found Ripper, a young bitser (a mix of a few breeds) that needed a good home. The pup was not what you might call handsome, but he was chock-full of character. They soon became inseparable.

After the training session had ended, Cassie and Ripper were picking up the last of the equipment when Cassie noticed a dog enter the park, one she hadn't seen before. She was a shaggy sheepdog, and Cassie thought she was gorgeous! Her owner was getting dragged along behind her.

'Whoa, girl, whoa,' called the boy, as he hopelessly tried to control his dog.

Cassie peered at the owner. He looked familiar. She jogged over to him. 'Hey, are you the new boy in 5W?'

The new boy looked embarrassed. 'Umm, yeah, I – whoa, Florence, heel, girl!' A moment later the sheepdog had jerked free of his owner and left him sprawled in

the grass as she took off after Henry the beagle, who was having a quiet sniff and dig under a huge acacia tree in the corner of the park.

'Great, just great,' said the boy, checking out a new hole in his school trousers.

Cassie thought it best to change the subject. 'I'm Cassie, and you're –?' she asked.

'Ben Stoppard.' He didn't make eye contact with Cassie. 'And I better go grab my . . .' He jogged off before even finishing the sentence.

Well, thought Cassie to herself. Both Ben and his dog needed some serious behaviour training!

Chapter Two

Later that evening, Cassie was helping out behind the counter of the family's deli while wrestling with her homework.

'Bye, Mrs P,' she said as she handed over the bag of groceries to the old woman. 'And remember, now that Cuddles has had the abscess lanced, she'll need to stay out of trouble and take it easy for a few days.'

Mrs Papandrea smiled at Cassie. 'Just what the nurse said too, dear.' She walked towards the exit. 'Good luck with your maths test.'

Cassie groaned and glanced back at her workbook. Why wasn't maths as fun as looking after animals?

'Which one's diameter and which is radius again, Gladiator?' she asked the cat draped over her lap. Gladiator was dreaming of chasing lizards and wasn't about to leave the dream for maths homework!

A man stepped up to the counter with a smile. 'Uh, I think radius is the length from the centre to the edge of the circle, and the diameter is the full length.'

Cassie grinned. 'That's right. Of course. I knew that.' She scrawled in her workbook. 'Oh, and thanks by the way,' she said, looking up. She immediately noticed he was wearing a shirt with an RSPCA logo on it. 'So, you're the new vet,' she said, 'I'm Cassie. I love animals . . . but I don't feel the same way about maths.'

The new vet smiled. 'No, I can't say I love maths either. I'm Dr Joe Stoppard. Nice to meet you, Cassie. My family and I have just moved here from Bendigo –'

'Stoppard? Oh, so you're Ben's dad?' asked Cassie, putting two and two together.

'That's right. Are you both in the same class?'

'Not the same class, but we're both in year five.'

'Well, I'm here to find something dinnerish.' He glanced around the shop, looking a little vague.

Cassie removed Gladiator from her lap and put him back in his basket before coming around from behind the counter. 'I'd suggest this bolognaise. It's my dad's special recipe,' she said, grabbing the container. 'Just add spaghetti!'

Dr Joe nodded. 'Great, and I guess I might –'

Cassie handed him a block of parmesan cheese and some garlic bread.

'Yes, that was exactly what I was . . .' He lost track of his thought as he reached into his jeans pocket and found only a scrunched-up handkerchief. 'Ah . . .' he said, looking flustered, 'I must have left my wallet next door at the surgery.'

'Don't worry, Dr Joe,' she said. 'You can drop in the money for your dinner next time you pass by.'

'Well, that's very kind of you, Cassie.' The vet smiled. 'Here I was thinking that a move to the big smoke would mean people were going to be less friendly,' he said.

'Oh no, Abbotts Hill is one of the friendliest neighbourhoods ever,' she said with great gusto. 'Everyone's super-nice, and there are lots of great pets too,' she added. 'I've even met your Old English sheepdog, Florence.'

Dr Joe groaned. 'Oh dear, does that mean she ran riot in the shop, or tried to eat your cat for breakfast?'

Cassie laughed. 'Not quite. And if she tried, I think Gladiator would put up a pretty good fight. I saw her down at the dog park. She does look like quite a handful.'

'Yes, people expect a vet to have well behaved pets,' he said. 'Sadly, that isn't always the case.'

'Well, she's totally gorgeous. Sheep-dogs are smart dogs and can be trained –'

She was interrupted by an annoyed Ben entering the shop. 'Dad, come on, I'm starving to death out . . .' He clocked

Cassie behind the counter. 'Oh, it's you again.'

Dr Joe turned and frowned at his son's tone.

'Yes, it's me again,' Cassie said, not pleased with his attitude either.

'Well, it was *lovely* to meet you, Cassie,' covered Dr Joe, still frowning at Ben. 'I'll drop the money in tomorrow morning on the way to work.'

'No problems. See you round,' said Cassie, as father and son left the shop.

'What is wrong with that rude boy?' mumbled Cassie. Gladiator opened half an eye in an 'I don't know and I don't much care' sort of way.

Cassie nodded. 'You're right. I don't care either.' But she was friendly with everyone in Abbotts Hill, and one boy wasn't going to upset her perfect track record!

Chapter Three

After school the next day, Ben and his dad were taking Florence for a walk to the dog park. 'So who are you sitting next to in class?'

Ben responded with a grunt. 'Don't know his name.'

His dad tried again. 'What would you

like for dinner tonight?'

Ben shrugged. 'I guess Mum's working late again?'

His dad nodded. 'Yes, Ben, you know your mother is working hard at her new job . . .'

Florence, sensing her owners were a little distracted, started wandering a little further ahead on her leash.

'Whatever,' said Ben rudely, kicking the ground with his toe.

'Oh, stop with the pity party, Ben,' said his dad, growing frustrated. 'She's a surgeon and she works long hours saving lives, and you need to get used to it!'

Meanwhile, Florence caught sight of an old ginger cat meandering around the front garden of a nearby house. *Hooray, a playmate*, she thought excitedly, and launched herself into the garden, yanking the lead from Ben's hand.

There was a large hiss and a YEOOOOOOWWWL, and a second later an old woman appeared at the front door, letting loose a howl of her own. 'Get that fluffball away from my Cuddles!'

Ben sprinted into the woman's front yard and tried to grab Florence, who was bounding around the base of an apple tree, yapping, with a big smile on her face.

Cuddles had scrambled up the tree. She was perched precariously on a branch that didn't look as if it could take the overweight cat's heft for too much longer. She was hissing down at Florence, who considered that encouragement and yapped some more.

'Ben, get Florence away from that cat,' Dr Joe yelled above the dog's barking.

'What do you think I'm trying to do?' responded Ben, trying to round up Florence, who was having too much fun to budge from under the tree.

The old lady was outraged. 'I'll have you know Cuddles has just had an operation. She's meant to be recuperating QUIETLY!' she yelped, cranking up the decibels over Florence's yaps.

Dr Joe noticed the old woman was starting to look more and more like her irate cat. 'I'm so sorry. Look, we'll have this under control in a minute . . .'

Just then, Cassie and Ripper rounded the corner on their way to the dog park. Cassie quickly observed the tense situation, put her fingers to her lips and let out a shrill whistle. Everyone stopped and turned in her direction.

With Florence's attention diverted away from Cuddles the cat, Ben was able to grab hold of her collar and pick up the lead. It had been dragged and twisted around what had probably been a pretty flowerbed. But now, with Florence's input, it looked more like a thoroughfare for a herd of clumsy emu.

Ben led Florence quickly out of Cuddles' gate and stood awkwardly on the footpath, looking as though he'd prefer to be teleported to another galaxy.

The cat glanced gratefully at Cassie, gave one more half-hearted hiss in Florence's direction, jumped down off the apple tree and galloped into the safety of her house.

'Don't worry, Mrs P, Cuddles will be fine,' reassured Cassie.

'I hope you're right, dear.' Mrs P shook her head. 'Really, dog owners should be more responsible!' She slammed her front door shut.

'Well, that's one way of meeting the neighbours,' Dr Joe said with a shrug, trying to make light of the situation.

Cassie giggled. 'I'd suggest hiding next time Mrs Papandrea comes into the vet clinic, Dr Joe. She and her cat have attitude to burn!'

'Dad, we better get going,' Ben suggested. For once in his life Ben wanted Florence to be pulling on the lead, but she was over making friends with Cassie's dog. *Typical.*

Cassie had not finished with the subdued new boy. 'Oh, Ben,' she said innocently. 'I was wondering if you and your dad were coming on the Million Paws Walk this weekend?'

Ben hesitated. 'Ah, I'm not sure. We have a lot on.'

Ben's dad raised an eyebrow. It was the first he'd heard of a busy weekend schedule.

Cassie continued with her plan of attack. 'I'm doing some lunchtime fundraising tomorrow, and you're welcome to help out if you want? I mean, I guess you'd be interested, seeing as your dad works for the RSPCA.'

'Ben, that would be great. It would give you a chance to meet some new kids,' chimed Dr Joe.

Ben gave his father a death stare. 'Yeah, um, we'll see.'

Cassie grinned. 'Okay, I'll be near the canteen after the lunch bell goes. See you there. Bye, Dr Joe. Come on, Ripper.'

Girl and dog walked purposefully off up the street.

Once they were out of earshot Ben mumbled, 'Thanks a lot, Dad!'

'Anytime, son,' Dr Joe replied, deciding to ignore his son's sarcastic tone.

Chapter Four

The morning of the Million Paws Walk, the Bannerman family were up early. Fundraising walks were taking place all over Australia, and the nearest one to the Bannermans' house was only about 15 minutes' drive away. Cassie's dad, Alex, had been preparing and cooking the family speciality, pastizzi, a delicious buttery pastry filled with ricotta. Cassie's mum, Samantha, was going to be in charge of a food stall at the park, feeding hungry pet owners, with proceeds going to the RSPCA. Cassie and her mum were at the park putting the final touches to the stall.

'A perfect autumn morning, Cass,' said Samantha, looking up at the clear blue sky.

Cass wasn't as interested in the weather as she was in all the dogs walking by. 'Oh, Mum, look at that super-cute retriever. And that pug? He must be mixed with some other breed. You don't normally see that type of colouration. Awww, so cute, those Cavalier King

Charles spaniels have matching tartan waistcoats!'

Cassie's mum couldn't keep up with her daughter's commentary. 'Cass, you take Ripper and do the walk. You're not going to be able to concentrate on selling food here today, that's for sure.'

Cass looked momentarily guilty.

Samantha shook her head. 'I don't expect you to, darling. You and Ripper have a fantastic time.'

Cassie looked at Ripper. 'Ready, boy?'

Ripper looked as if he was about to do cartwheels with excitement, he was so ready. The pair took off into the crowd.

'Bye, Mum. We'll come back after the

walk for leftover pastizzi, Cassie called over her shoulder.

'I'll do my best to save you one,' said Samantha doubtfully as she noted the swarms of people and dogs arriving at the park.

As she was lining up to begin the walk, Cassie found a couple of school friends in the crowd, Ramona and Sal. They were identical twins who had matching brown Labradors.

'Hi, Cassie, hi, Ripper,' the twins said in unison.

'Hi, girls. Hey, it looks like Judy and

Jasper are already having fun.' Cassie smiled as she gave each dog a pat.

'Well, they made a beeline straight to the doggy gelato stand as soon as we arrived . . .' Ramona started off.

'Behaving just like typical Labradors always do!' finished up Sal.

Cassie nodded. 'Hey, thanks again for your help with the fundraising cupcake stall the other day,' said Cassie.

'Anytime. How much money did you raise?' asked Ramona.

'Over seventy dollars. It's my most successful year yet!'

'Hey, there's that new boy,' said Ramona, pointing over Cassie's head. 'What's his name again?'

Cassie caught sight of a large hairy mop

racing in her direction, with Ben Stoppard trying but failing to stop the charge.

Ripper gave a welcoming bark hello, and Florence smelled Ripper's bottom in appreciation.

Ben looked guilty. 'Ah, hi,' he said, blushing at the girls.

'Ramona, Sal, this is Ben.'

'Um, sorry I didn't help with your fundraising the other day . . .' Ben said to Cassie.

'Oh, so you're the boy who didn't turn up,' said Sal with a mock grimace. 'Don't worry, we did all the hard work without you.'

Cassie elbowed Sal in the ribs and said to Ben, 'Don't worry. She's joking.' She turned to the girls. 'Ben's dad is the new vet at the RSPCA and he's awesome!' said Cassie.

Ramona raised an eyebrow. 'Ben's awesome, is he?' She turned to her twin.

Sal giggled. 'Hello, awesome Ben,' she said, fluttering her eyelashes.

Ben blushed harder.

Cassie just shook her head. 'You two are trouble! You know that I meant his *dad* is awesome.'

'Sure you did,' said Sal. 'See you two later!' The twins and their dogs trotted off.

Cassie turned to Ben. 'Don't worry about those two. They're the class clowns.' She looked around. 'Are your parents here?'

'Mum's working at the hospital, but

Dad's helping with the free vet checks at the tent over there,' he said, pointing to a row of tents further up the path on the left.

'Well, Ripper and Florence look as though they want to keep walking together. Okay with you?' asked Cassie.

'Sure but, you know, I'm not anywhere near as "awesome" as my dad,' said Ben with a small smile.

'Hang on,' said Cassie, looking shocked. 'Do that again!'

Ben looked alarmed. 'What?'

Cassie frowned. 'I think I saw you smile. First time ever. Are you feeling ill or something?'

Ben smiled again. 'Maybe.'

The two children and the two dogs began the walk together, quickly getting enveloped in the large crowd of dog owners and their pet canines.

Some kids looked forward to their birthdays or to school holidays, but days like this were the highlight of Cassie's year.

What could be better than a walk in the great outdoors on a beautiful day with thousands of gorgeous dogs?!

Chapter Five

Cassie's enthusiasm was contagious, and Ben soon realised he was beginning to like the girl he'd first thought was too pushy. She was fun and obviously *loved* animals. And his dog had a serious crush on Ripper. It was embarrassing, but there was nothing Ben could do about it.

Frankly, Ripper was such a cool dog that Ben didn't blame Florence. He was super-obedient, not like you-know-who, he trotted around like he owned the place and he did the most awesome tricks.

Right now, Ripper was having a free mobile dog-wash, standing still and proud. Florence, on the other hand . . .

Cassie was bent over double, laughing. 'Florence, you look like . . .' She dissolved into giggles and couldn't continue.

The poor dog-washer was trying her best to stay good-natured, but Florence's constant moving and shaking was making the dog-washer the wetter and soapier of the two of them. And it only got worse when it came time to dry her. 'Aaaarooooow, aaaroooow,'

Florence yowled, competing with the noise of the blow-dryer.

Ripper, even while getting his short hair dried, remained dignified, looking over at Florence now and then to make sure his new friend wasn't in need of assistance.

Finally the two dogs finished their grooming, and the four of them could continue along the walk. Of course, Florence took about two seconds to find a mud puddle to douse herself in, undoing all the fine work the dog-washer had done.

'Florence, you are a total walking disaster zone,' complained Ben good-naturedly.

'Oh, that's not true at all,' defended Cassie, giving the big dog a pat on the back and earning a happy tail-wag in response.

'Haaa! Check that one out, Ben. There's a Jack Russell dressed as Spiderman.'

'Okay, that's good, but not as cool as that Staffy-cross dressed like a vampire,' said Ben, pointing at a dog wearing a black cape and an evil expression.

Cassie nodded. 'He certainly has the teeth for it.'

They were ambling along happily when a woman's high-pitched cry disrupted the happy crowd. 'Maxxieeee! Maxie, come back, baby!'

Cassie and Ben searched the crowd for the source of the cry. Cassie spotted the woman further up the path that led into the more forested part of the walk. She was running out of the crowd after a tearaway little ball of mischief that disappeared into the trees.

'Let's see if we can help.' Cassie didn't wait for a reply from Ben, and she and Ripper began walking fast, weaving around other walkers as they made their way over to the woman.

Ben and Florence followed, trying not to lose them.

Cassie and Ripper easily caught up to a woman in her twenties, brandishing a mobile phone. 'Maxie, Maxie, come back!' She put her phone to her ear. 'Sorry, I'll have to call you back,' she said and hung up.

'Hi, would you like us to help?' asked Cassie.

The woman glanced at Ripper with

a frown. 'Oh no, I don't want that animal anywhere near my little Maxie.' She then proceeded to ignore Cassie and get the attention of a male passerby who was walking a miniature poodle.

'Excuse me,' she said. 'Could you help me retrieve my naughty puppy?' Her phone beeped. 'Oh, hang on, I'll just answer this text message first.'

Cassie turned to Ripper, whispering, 'She thinks a miniature poodle can do a better retrieval job than you?'

Ripper looked back incredulously. Some humans made no sense at all!

Chapter Six

Meanwhile Maxie the naughty puppy was having the time of his life. While his owner was on her fourth phone call of the day, the pup had decided to run like the wind. Maxie's owner hadn't got around to buying a proper lead, and the pretty but totally impractical ribbon she'd been using instead frayed and broke when Maxie made his bid for freedom.

He was soon dodging large paws, small paws, big feet, little feet, clown feet and walking sticks. He'd become tangled in a couple of leads and legs, but each time he had managed to wriggle his way free before there was an all-out disaster.

This was turning out to be the best day of Maxie's short life.

Maxie's owner, on the other hand, was not having the best day of her life. One of the heels of her high-heeled sandals had snapped off and she was limping through the crowds, still with her phone to her ear, trying to catch up with her pup.

Ben and Florence had caught up with

Cassie and Ripper. Cassie turned to Ben, pink in the face. 'She said she didn't want our help, because my dog was not the right breed, or some rubbish,' said Cassie, still mightily annoyed by the woman's attitude.

Ben shook his head sympathetically. 'Well, Ripper, I think you and Cassie need to show that lady a thing or two about what kind of dog you really are!'

Ripper stood to attention. He knew he was up to the task.

Cassie looked at Ben, nodding. 'You're right. Who cares what she thinks? That little puppy needs our help.' She glanced over at Florence, who was smiling at Ripper like a love-struck teenager. 'All our help. C'mon, team!' The four headed off determinedly, swerving through the crowds.

Up ahead, in a small picnic area off from the walk's main thoroughfare, was a gleaming doggie gelato stand. There were three or four dogs hungrily licking up the last remains of their treat, tails wagging fiercely in appreciation. Their owners were relaxing nearby, some with a coffee in their hand, enjoying the slight breeze and general ambience of the day.

Maxie was beginning to realise this free-range running business was hard work and, sniffing the air, decided that what a hot dog needed after a long run was a nice cool gelato. Maxie didn't know what doggie gelato tasted like, but he knew he wanted to find out. He veered to the right, tripping over a few more legs, and headed towards the picnic area, full speed ahead!

Chapter Seven

Moments later, it was as though a small, four-pawed tornado had passed through the picnic area: the gelato stand had tipped right over; an ever-growing lake of gelato was spreading over the concreted area, which was causing an ever-growing number of dogs to detour off the path and pull their owners towards what looked like a delicious mid-walk treat.

The poor gelato man was face first on the ground with a naughty little puppy chewing on his apron. And there was only one dog to blame for the whole disaster.

'Maxie, little Maxie!' called out the puppy's owner, still a few hundred metres away from the picnic area and oblivious to the calamity that was just ahead of her.

Cassie and Ben reached the crime scene first, and Ben made a grab for the pup. Unfortunately, Maxie had not finished having fun, and he squirmed out of Ben's hands, took a quick lick of the gelato lake and continued off course, towards the bushland behind the picnic area.

'Follow that dog!' cried Cassie, and Florence and Ripper were only too happy to obey the order.

'That is one slippery character!' said Ben, still holding onto Florence's lead as he puffed along after the dogs. He was slightly embarrassed to note Cassie wasn't breathless in the least as she jogged along beside him, effortlessly keeping pace . . . although she did have a concerned look on her face. Perhaps looking effortless took a lot of concentration?

'We have to catch the pup before he disappears too far into the bushland,' said Cassie.

'Why? Because there's a bunyip in there?' joked Ben, secretly enjoying himself for the first time in weeks.

Cassie frowned. 'No. I'd be fine with a bunyip,' she said. 'It's the four-lane highway on the other side of the bushland that I'm worried about.'

Ben realised this was no longer a game. The runaway puppy's life was now in danger.

The rescue party increased their speed.

Maxie was starting to tire. His little legs had never carried him so far at such a pace. Now that he was travelling away from the large crowds, the game wasn't so much fun. He was starting to miss his owner and was a little annoyed she hadn't managed to keep up. Slowing down to a trot, he sniffed the wind, taking in the different scents of his unfamiliar surroundings. He was starting to feel a little scared. He stifled a yawn and then stood on something sharp. Oowww. Not nice!

A hundred metres behind Maxie, the four friends were gaining on the puppy. Cassie noticed him slowing and she tapped Ben on the arm.

'I'm going to take Ripper around the long way and try to get in front of the puppy. You and Florence keep on going straight after him, but keep it slow and steady, okay?'

Ben was swallowing great gulps of air now. He was seriously unfit. Cassie's instruction not to go fast sounded like very good news to him. He made the okay symbol rather than wasting precious breath on speaking.

Cassie waved goodbye and whistled to Ripper, and the two veered off to the left.

Chapter Eight

Ben and Florence were easily gaining ground on the puppy, who was visibly flagging now. He didn't look as if he had any more energy to run, which was exactly how Ben felt too! Florence and Ben slowed to a walking pace, Florence not so keen to run now that Ripper wasn't with her.

They walked slowly, trying to make sure they offered no further excitement for the tired puppy.

They were only a few metres away from the pup when a noisy golf buggy advertising doggy shampoo drove up, with Maxie's owner driving and talking on the phone at the same time. 'I know, can you believe it? The guy just handed me the keys to the golf buggy. He was sooo nice. Oh, there's my dog. Better go.'

Ben couldn't believe it. Did that woman ever stop using her mobile phone?

Instead of turning the key into the 'off' position, she revved the buggy by accident, which frightened Maxie and he took off further into the dense bush.

'Oh, how annoying,' said Maxie's owner. She hopped off the golf buggy with her broken shoes. 'Now I'm going to get all dirty.'

She walked a couple of paces and her phone beeped. She started texting again.

Ben and Florence left her to it and continued into the bushland after the runaway pup.

Maxie was almost through the woodland now and saw the busy road up ahead. If he could get to the other side, perhaps he could find a nice snack and a quiet place to

lie down. His foot hurt and he wasn't having fun any more.

Suddenly a girl appeared in front of him, talking softly. 'Hey, Maxie, you're looking tired and hungry, little guy.'

She reached out a hand gently to Maxie, and he gave it a sniff. YUM! The girl had one of his favourite doggy treats in her hand!

Maxie gulped it in a second and looked up at Cassie with his big eyes.

Cassie seemed to read Maxie's mind. 'How about two more? And that's it.' She handed them over, and once Maxie had finished, she picked him up gently. He collapsed into her arms, happy that his little adventure was over.

Once Maxie was comfortable, Ripper came out from behind a nearby tree, on his best behaviour.

Cassie patted her dog. 'Let's go reunite Maxie with his owner, Ripper!'

Ripper charged ahead and found Ben and Florence first.

'Hey, Ben,' said Cassie quietly, so as not to wake the puppy. 'Can you take a look at Maxie's paw? He was limping when I found him.'

Ben only took a moment to discover the thistle and removed it so gently that Maxie didn't even stir.

Maxie's owner arrived to see the two children taking good care of her pup.

'I'm sorry I was rude to you earlier,' she

said, looking guilty, as Cassie handed the exhausted dog back to his owner. 'I still have a lot to learn about looking after a puppy.'

Cassie shrugged, giving Ripper a pat. 'Ripper was a bit of a tearaway when he was a pup too.'

Ripper smiled his enthusiastic, toothy smile. Maxie's owner looked a little alarmed, but tried to hide it.

'Maxie's the right age to take to puppy training classes. And it would help to get him a proper lead,' suggested Cassie politely.

The owner's phone rang and she nodded her thanks before turning away to speak. 'Yes, little Maxie's back with me now. Drama over . . .' She walked away, continuing the conversation.

'It would also help if you weren't on the phone all the time,' mentioned Ben cheekily, once she was out of hearing range.

Florence barked heartily in agreement!

Chapter Nine

The rest of the Million Paws Walk went off without a hitch. Dogs had a great time, owners had a great time, the doggie gelato stand was back in business and RSPCA supporters raised thousands of dollars that would help animals at shelters all over Australia.

Ben had taken Ripper and Florence for one more stroll around the park on his own while Cassie and her mum packed up the pastizzi stand.

When Dr Joe had finished with the vet checks, he made his way over to the Bannerman food stand with his wife, Veronica. She had just come from her shift at the hospital.

'Oh, those pastizzi smell so good!' said Veronica.

'Veronica, I'd like to introduce you to the Bannerman family,' said Dr Joe.

Veronica shook hands with Cassie's mum and gave Cassie a warm smile. 'So you're the family responsible for making the best bolognaise I've ever tasted,' enthused Veronica.

'That's them, all right,' Dr Joe said.

Veronica said to Samantha, 'Your cooking is reason enough to move interstate.'

Samantha beamed. There was nothing she liked more than people appreciating her family's cooking. 'Ah, it's my husband, Alex, who is the master chef in the family. Here,' she said, passing over the last pastizzi. 'Enjoy!'

A moment after Veronica had taken her first delicious bite, Ben came rushing over excitedly with the two dogs. 'Mum, you made it!'

Veronica gave her son a quick hug. 'Sorry I couldn't get here sooner,' she said.

Ben grinned. 'You're just in time. You're

not going to believe this, but Florence has learnt her first trick – with the help of superdog Ripper.'

Cassie grinned. 'He'll get a big head if you go around calling him superdog!'

Both Ben's parents looked sceptical. 'Our dog Florence?' said Ben's mum.

'The four-legged fluffy mop who has never followed a single instruction in her whole life?' said Ben's dad.

'Prepare to be amazed!' Ben said in his best magician's voice.

He brought Florence out into the open space in front of where his parents and the Bannermans were standing, and gave the command. 'Florence, stay!'

Florence stayed.

Ben turned to Ripper. 'Ripper, you know what to do.'

Ripper backed up a few metres, steadied himself and trotted up to Florence.

Florence wagged her tail.

The Stoppards looked at each other, puzzled.

Ripper lifted his front right paw off the ground, still looking at Florence.

Florence dropped and rolled over on her back, legs in the air.

Ripper put his paw back on the ground, and Florence rolled back onto her feet.

The Stoppards and the Bannermans applauded.

Cassie laughed. 'That's awesome, Ben!

Who knew Florence could take instruction so well?!'

Ben laughed and gave his dog a big hug. 'When Ripper's around, Florence is on her best behaviour!'

Cassie gave Ripper a hug too. 'Why don't you bring Florence along to training next Tuesday at the dog park? She'll love it!'

'It's a deal,' Ben replied as he shook hands with Cassie.

Ripper raised his paw to Ben and Ben shook Ripper's hand too.

Cassie laughed. 'Consider it a double deal.'

ABOUT THE RSPCA

The RSPCA is the country's best known and most respected animal welfare organisation. The first RSPCA in Australia was formed in Victoria in 1871, and the organisation is now represented by RSPCAs in every state and territory.

The RSPCA's mission is to prevent cruelty to animals by actively promoting their care and protection. It is a not-for-profit charity that is firmly based in the Australian community, relying upon the support of individuals, businesses and organisations to survive and continue its vital work.

Every year, RSPCA shelters throughout Australia accept over 150,000 sick, injured or abandoned animals from the community. The RSPCA believes that every animal is entitled to the Five Freedoms:

Fact File

- freedom from hunger and thirst (ready access to fresh water and a healthy, balanced diet)
- freedom from discomfort, including accommodation in an appropriate environment that has shelter and a comfortable resting area
- freedom from pain, injury or disease through prevention or rapid diagnosis and providing veterinary treatment when required

- freedom to express normal behaviour, including sufficient space, proper facilities and company of the animal's own kind

and

- freedom from fear and distress through conditions and treatment that avoid suffering.

THE MILLION PAWS WALK

The Million Paws Walk is the RSPCA's major national fundraiser. Every May, over 80,000 people and 40,000 pets hit the pavement to raise much needed funds for the RSPCA.

Visit http://www.millionpawswalk.com.au to register for the next event!

CARING FOR YOUR DOG

Dogs are very smart and make loyal and fun friends. Remember that the best way to teach a dog is through kindness and rewarding good behaviour.

What do dogs eat?

We can buy pet food from the supermarket or from our vets that is specially made to meet the needs of our dogs and make sure they stay healthy. Healthy food is especially important for puppies, mothers who have just had puppies and older dogs. Get your

parents to look for the words 'balanced' or 'complete' on the packaging to make sure your dog is getting everything he needs.

Fact File

How can we make dogs comfortable?
Dogs need a cosy, dry place to rest and sleep — one that will protect them from the sun, wind and rain. Their beds should be soft and warm and cleaned every week, just like our own beds!

How do dogs talk to each other?
When your puppy is very young, between 4 and 18 weeks of age, he needs to get used to meeting different people and playing with other dogs. A great way to do this is to take your new family member to puppy preschool classes. You and your dog will learn lots of new things and he will have a chance to meet other dogs. You and your parents will learn how to teach your puppy manners.

How do dogs keep fit and healthy?
Walking, fetching balls and playing frisbee are great ways to exercise dogs. If dogs are being taken outside their homes, they need to be on leads. Your dog should get some exercise at least twice a day.

Fact File

To make sure your pet dog is healthy, they must visit the vet at least once a year for a check-up. You should also take your dog to the vet if he seems unwell and is vomiting a lot, coughing, sleeping all the time or not eating.

How do I make sure my dog is safe and does not get lost?

Your garden should have good fencing to make sure your dog cannot get out. Your dog must also wear a collar with a name tag. This will have your phone number on it so if he does get lost people will know who he belongs to.

You can also have a microchip put under your dog's coat. A microchip is a very clever little device that the vet puts under the dog's skin with a needle. The microchip is as big as a grain of rice and doesn't hurt him at all, but it means if he does get lost and his collar falls off, the vet or the RSPCA can run a scanner over his neck and it will tell them who he belongs to. Your dog will always find his way back home with a microchip!

Fact File

How long do dogs live for?
This depends on the size of the dog, but most live around 8-14 years. A small dog can live much longer.

What does my dog need?
• Someone to love and look after them for their whole life.
• Friendship: to be with other dogs or people and not to be left alone for too long.
• Healthy food every day.
• Fresh, cool, clean water every day.
• Regular visits to the vet for their injections and medicine.
• Regular walks (at least once a day).
• A well-fenced garden to play in.
• Raw bones or hide toys to chew on to keep teeth and gums healthy. This is just like brushing their teeth!
• Regular brushing. Dogs with long hair need to be brushed every day. Some dogs need to have haircuts regularly, just like we do!
• Someone to care for them when you are away.

Fact File

- Never to be left alone in a car.
- To be desexed.
- A collar and name tag.
- A microchip.
- To be registered with the local council.
- Training.
- A clean environment.
- A place sheltered from the sun, wind and rain, with a bed and their own blanket.
- To be trained using kindness.

WANT MORE

RSPCA

Animal Tales?

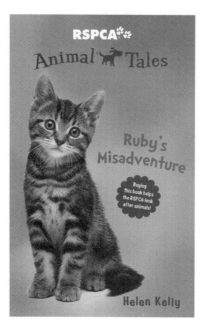

Read on for an extract from
Book Two:
RUBY'S MISADVENTURE!

Chapter One

'Three sleepovers in a row! It's going to be just like we're sisters!' said Sarah.

Sarah was beside herself with excitement and Cassie let her go on without interruption. She was excited too, of course; it was going to be a wonderful few days.

School had finished and the girls were

passing by the park on their way home, just as they did every day. But today was different. Today was the day that they had both been looking forward to for weeks.

Sarah's parents had been married for eleven years and had decided that this year it was time for them to celebrate their wedding anniversary in style. They had booked themselves into a hotel on the beach for three whole days and children were not allowed!

'I still can't believe Mum let me stay here with you, instead of going to Gran's with the boys. It's going to be so quiet without them!' Sarah sighed. 'So, what shall we do first, Cassie? As my older and wiser *sister*, I think you should decide.'

'Mmmm. I am two months older and y'know, that really does make me very, very wise.' Cassie adopted her most thoughtful expression and pondered. 'How about starting with a milkshake?' This was a common suggestion from Cassie. Her mum and dad ran the local deli in Abbotts Hill and made the best milkshakes for miles around.

'Perfect!' agreed Sarah.

'Then we could take Ripper down to the park for a run. You know Mark from school? His family have just adopted a tiny pug from the RSPCA. He might be there. He's called –'

Cassie came to an abrupt stop. Sarah heard a garbled *aaarghh* and turned around to see her friend flat on the floor with a large black-and-white dog on top of her! Sarah didn't know what to do. But then she realised that Cassie was laughing so hard that she could hardly breathe. Sarah exhaled with relief. Clearly this dog was friend, not foe.

Cassie managed to get herself into a sitting position but was still full of giggles.

'Calm down, Florence! Yes, it's great to see you too. Now sit!'

The dog sat obediently and Cassie managed to get to her feet, straightening her hair, her school-bag and her slobbered-on face all in one smooth movement.

'So this is a friend of yours?' asked Sarah.

'Sarah, meet Florence and –' Cassie glanced back in the direction Florence had come from '– you know Ben Stoppard from school.'

A very embarrassed-looking Ben ran up to them.

'Hi, Ben. Lost something?' asked Cassie.

'No!' He spluttered, staring furtively back the way he'd come. 'No, it's just that Florence got away from me. You know what she's like.'

He was breathless from running across the park. 'She must have seen you. She just took off! Are you okay?' Ben regained his breath and flicked his floppy hair back as he picked up the end of his dog's lead. Florence smiled beautifully at each of them and continued to sit.

'I'm fine!' said Cassie. 'No harm done, though some doggy breath-freshener wouldn't go amiss. Eau de Dog Breath is definitely *not* my favourite fragrance.'

'What are you two up to?' asked Ben as he looked back into the park again.

'We're just heading home for a milkshake,' said Cassie. 'Sarah's staying with me for three days and we have some serious planning to do for tonight!'

'That sounds great!' said Ben. 'What's the flavour of the day?'

Both Cassie and Sarah stopped and stared at him.

'Let me rephrase that for you,' said Cassie. '*Sarah and I* are going home to plan *our super-girly sleepover* over a milkshake. Just so there's no confusion, that is, *a sleepover for girls*, talking about *girl's stuff*. Maybe we'll see you later back here? I promised Mrs Stephens that I'll take Rusty out for a walk.'

Ben was still looking uneasily over his

shoulder and seemed keen to leave the park quickly.

'I'll just join you for the milkshake bit, then. Come on, let's go.'

Ben was behaving very strangely and the girls weren't sure his ears were working properly either. He was definitely up to something.

Cassie and Sarah glanced back into the park to see what he might be avoiding, but could see nothing except a gaggle of small children and lots of dogs.

'Okay,' they agreed. 'But only for the milkshake bit!'

RSPCA

Animal

AVAILABLE NOW

Tales

COLLECT THEM ALL

COMING SEPTEMBER 2012